THE JOLLY MON

by Jimmy Buffett & Savannah Jane Buffett

Illustrated by Lambert Davis

HARCOURT BRACE JOVANOVICH, PUBLISHERS

San Diego   New York   London

HBJ

Requests for permission to make copies of
any part of the work should be mailed to:
Copyrights and Permissions Department,
Harcourt Brace Jovanovich, Publishers,
Orlando, Florida 32887.

Library of Congress Cataloging-in-Publication Data

Buffett, Jimmy.
  The Jolly Mon.
  Summary: Relates the adventures of a fisherman who
finds a magic guitar floating in the Caribbean Sea.
  [1. Fairy tales. 2. Caribbean Area–Fiction]
I. Buffett, Savannah Jane. II. Davis, Lambert, ill.
III. Title.
PZ8.B87Jo   1988   [E]   87-8573
ISBN 0-15-240530-5

DEFGH

The paintings in this book were done in acrylics
on D'Arches 140 lb. cold press watercolor paper.

The text type was set in Cloister.

The display type was set in Caslon Antique Italic.

Color separations were made by Bright Arts (Hong Kong) Ltd.

Composed by Thompson Type, San Diego, California

Printed and bound by Tien Wah Press, Singapore

Production supervision by Warren Wallerstein and Rebecca Miller

Designed by Michael Farmer

To all the people on all the islands in the Caribbean
and all the dolphins in the sea below

—J. B.
S.J.B.

To my family and friends

—L. D.

Storytellers' Note

It seems that pirates have been throwing musicians into the oceans since the beginning of time, and thankfully dolphins have been around just as long to pluck us out so that we can continue to sing. As I told my daughter, Savannah Jane, a bad review today is nothing compared to a bad review in the old days. The poet and musician Arion seems to be the first musician to have gotten the proverbial "hook" as he was traveling and singing his way through Italy around 625 B.C. He was saved by a dolphin who liked his music a lot more than the pirates, who seemed to have different taste and threw him overboard.

Dolphins have struck a mystical chord with artists and other people long before Flipper popularized the relationship on television. The sight of a school of dolphins crisscrossing in front of my boat, coupled with the sight of the constellation Orion appearing overhead every night, brings me joy and lessens the fears of voyaging on the lonely ocean. I have also found that life on the remote and beautiful islands of the Caribbean is enviable for the simplicity and friendliness of people who depend on the sea for their livelihood.

These are the views of the world that I have tried to expose my daughter to from the time she took her first steps on the deck of a ketch en route to St. Barth's. Savannah Jane and I have been lucky enough to share many such days and nights in the West Indies. And if you are never able to really go to a place like Bananaland, we hope we can bring it to you for a while, for that is what a story is all about.

—*Jimmy Buffett*
Savannah Jane Buffett
Maui, Hawaii

ONCE UPON A TIME, in the middle of the Caribbean Sea, there was a little island called Bananaland.

Had it not been for the threat of pirate ships, Bananaland would have been the most peaceful place on earth. The islanders grew up healthy and strong from eating bananas they pulled from trees in the rain forest and fish they caught on the shores of Snapper Bay.

Each day at dawn, the fishermen carried frying pans down to the beach. As the sun came up, they sang a song so magical that the fish jumped out of the sea and into their frying pans. The fishermen kept only what they needed and threw the rest back into Snapper Bay.

One fisherman had a sweeter voice than all the rest. They called him the Jolly Mon. He could sing more fish out of the ocean than anyone.

One morning, when the Jolly Mon went to the beach to sing for his breakfast, he discovered a beautiful guitar floating in Snapper Bay. Quickly he waded into the water and pulled it out.

It was a magnificent instrument. Conch pearls lined the neck, and coral starfish and seahorses glistened around the sound hole. Painted on the back, a white dolphin swam through stars made of sparkling diamonds.

When the Jolly Mon saw these stars, he recognized the constellation Orion. Below, inscribed in gold, were these words:

I come from the ocean with songs of the sea;
No lesson for learning, just play upon me.
Now go make your music in lands near and far;
Orion protects you wherever you are.

The Jolly Mon had never played a guitar before, but the moment his fingers touched the strings, he knew how to play. He was amazed. It was as if his hands had a mind of their own. He played and played and played.

People from all over the island heard the music and ran to Snapper Bay. The Jolly Mon told them what had happened. Soon Good King Jones, the ruler of all Bananaland, arrived. When he heard the story, he declared that the people of Bananaland should build a boat so his dear friend the Jolly Mon could follow the instructions on the magic guitar and share the happiness of his music with other islands.

The people of Bananaland brought mahogany logs from the rain forest and cut them into planks that the boatbuilders shaped into a beautiful hull. The fishermen made sails from their best canvas and painted the white dolphin on the mainsail. After the work was done each day, the Jolly Mon studied the night sky and watched the stars of Orion rise in the east and travel across the heavens. These were the stars he would steer by.

When the boat was finished, Good King Jones declared a holiday. All the people of Bananaland came to Snapper Bay to wish the Jolly Mon well. Princess Marigold, the king's lovely daughter, broke a bottle of coconut milk on the shiny new bow.

"I christen thee *Orion*," the king said, "in honor of the stars that will guide thee. Take our beloved Jolly Mon and his magic guitar to spread joy wherever he goes, and return him safely to us."

The princess gave the Jolly Mon the royal spyglass to watch for pirates and a purple scarf for good luck. Then the Jolly Mon raised the mainsail and headed out to sea.

The stars shone brightly, and the wind was fair. It took the Jolly Mon far, far away.

From Pumpkin Island to Parrot Key, from Mango Bay to Lemonland, the Jolly Mon sang. The people of the islands loved to see him come, and they were sad to see him go. They brought him gifts and things to eat and books to read as he made his way through the islands. A few times, the Jolly Mon spotted pirates in the distance, but the *Orion* was so swift the pirates couldn't follow.

One day as the Jolly Mon sailed along, a delicious scent of fresh-baked coconut floated by on the breeze. He turned the *Orion* in the direction of the wonderful aroma, and that afternoon he spotted the island that smelled so good. He lifted his spyglass. People on the beach were beckoning him ashore.

It was the loveliest island he had ever seen. Thousands of coconut trees lined pink beaches, and he made his way up the channel toward a small village on the shore.

The people of Coconut Island had heard about the Jolly Mon and his magic guitar. They had waited and watched for the ship with the dolphin sail. Every day they had baked coconut cakes, hoping the smell would hurry the Jolly Mon to their island. They were the friendliest people he had met on his long journey.

The Jolly Mon stayed a long time on Coconut Island and sang every song he knew. When he couldn't think of any more, he just made up new songs on the spot.

But one day a ship brought sad news from Bananaland. Good King Jones had died. Princess Marigold missed the Jolly Mon greatly and needed him to return home to cheer up the people of Bananaland.

The Jolly Mon was very sad when he heard of the death of his friend. That afternoon, the people of Coconut Island filled the *Orion* with fish and fruit and bade the Jolly Mon a fond farewell. They waved to him from the beaches as the boat with the white dolphin on its mainsail disappeared into the horizon.

The Jolly Mon had crossed the entire Caribbean Sea on his journey, and he missed his people and his own little island. So he put up all the sails the *Orion* could carry, and now he headed for home as fast as the wind would take him.

One night, as he studied the stars, a strange light flickered ahead of him. He steered for the light, and as he got closer, the Jolly Mon saw that it wasn't a light at all. It was a burning ship, and cries of "Help! Help!" filled the air.

The Jolly Mon bravely steered close to the ship, ready to rescue the stranded crew.

Suddenly, fierce-looking strangers leaped onto the deck of the *Orion* and surrounded the Jolly Mon as he stood by the wheel. The ship wasn't really afire—it was a trick. The Jolly Mon had been captured by One-Eyed Rosy and her gang, the most feared pirates on the Caribbean Sea.

They tied him up and set about the *Orion* looking for valuables. One-Eyed Rosy knew all about the Jolly Mon.

"People," she sneered, "were not meant to be as happy as you make them." She put her cutlass to the Jolly Mon's throat.

Just then, one of the pirates came up from below, clutching the magic guitar. He tried to pry off the diamonds and pearls, but the gems wouldn't loosen. The pirates tried to smash the guitar, but it would not break.

"My guitar has powers of its own," the Jolly Mon told One-Eyed Rosy. "It should not be abused."

This made the pirates so furious they dragged the Jolly Mon to the bow of the *Orion*. "It's a watery grave for you!" one of them shouted.

They were about to throw him into the sea when One-Eyed Rosy stopped them. She shoved the guitar at the Jolly Mon.

"Play," she ordered.

The Jolly Mon put his trembling hands on the strings. The power took over, and he sang:

> *Under the heavens and under the sea,*
> *There's a friend I don't know, who holds the right key—*

The Jolly Mon's voice was so sweet it made One-Eyed Rosy's blood boil with anger.

"That's quite enough, Mister Jolly Mon," she yelled. "You've sung your last song!"

The pirates yanked the guitar away from the Jolly Mon. They wrapped him in chains and tied an anchor to his feet. Then One-Eyed Rosy pushed him into the sea.

As the Jolly Mon sank to the bottom, he thought about Princess Marigold and Bananaland. He would never see them again.

He could not free himself from the chains, and he was almost out of breath when a sudden swirl of bubbles made it possible for him to breathe underwater. He thought he was either dead or dreaming, but then he saw the dolphin. It was the same white dolphin that was painted on the guitar, and it untangled the Jolly Mon's chains and freed him. Together they rose to the surface in time to see the pirates towing away the *Orion*.

"People *were* meant to be as happy as you make them," said the dolphin, sliding beneath the Jolly Mon. "My name is Albion," he said. "I have come to take you home. Climb on board, and don't let go."

The long journey home on the dolphin's back took so much strength that the Jolly Mon was barely alive when Albion finally laid him on the shores of Snapper Bay. He was ill for many days, and when he could speak again, his first words were of the dolphin.

"Albion . . ." he said.

Princess Marigold came to his side. "Albion saved your life and led us to One-Eyed Rosy. Now her band of cutthroats are locked up where they can do no harm."

"But my guitar . . . my boat," moaned the Jolly Mon.

"Enough," said the princess. "Drink this jasmine tea."

Then Princess Marigold took the Jolly Mon by the hand and led him down to the shores of Snapper Bay.

The Jolly Mon looked, rubbed his eyes, and started to laugh with joy. There, sitting at anchor in the bay, was the *Orion,* dancing lightly on the waves. And leaning against a palm tree on the beach was the magic guitar.

The Jolly Mon turned the guitar over, but the painting of the white dolphin had disappeared. "Albion—" he cried.

"I'm right here," a familiar voice replied, and there was Albion, splashing in shallow water. "Yes, Jolly Mon, you have brought happiness to all of the islands, but now it is time for you to stay home. Princess Marigold and the people of Bananaland need you. They have chosen you to be their new king. Rule well, and if you need me, all you have to do is sing."

Albion dove beneath the waves. A few seconds later, he leaped out of the sea and did not come down. He flew up into the night, and his shadow passed in front of the silver moon that hung over Snapper Bay. Then he disappeared into the sky, heading toward Orion.

The Jolly Mon waved good-bye. And then he picked up his guitar to play:

> *I come from the ocean with songs of the sea;*
> *No lesson for learning, just play upon me.*
> *Now go make your music in lands near and far,*
> *Orion protects you wherever you are.*

The island people say that the Jolly Mon lived a long and happy life. He sang and played his beautiful guitar, and he ruled Bananaland with wisdom. Sometimes he sailed the *Orion* to see his friends in other places across the Caribbean Sea. From Coconut Island to Parrot Key, from Mango Bay to Lemonland, they loved to see him come, and they were sad to see him go.

Legend has it that when he was very, very old, the Jolly Mon sang his last song for Albion, who came back and took him up into the sky. And now when the island people wish upon a star, they see the dolphin and the Jolly Mon and his magic guitar.

Jolly Mon Sing

by Jimmy Buffett, Will Jennings,
and Michael Utley

Verses:

1. There is a tale that the is-land peo-ple tell. Don't care
2. wanted him to sing on the is-land near and far. He al-
3. making his way home on a dark and storm-y night when he

if it is true 'cause I love it so well.
ways found his way by O-ri-on luck-y star. He'd tell
heard a cry for help, and he saw a flash-ing light. When he

Jol-ly Mon sang for his sup-per ev-'ry night. The peo-
them of their joys, he'd tell them of their woes. They'd love
reached the o-ther boat and of-fered them a hand, they said

-ple fed him well 'cause he trea-ted them so right.
to see him come. They'd hate to see him go.
give us all your car-go as they took a pi-rate stand.

Chorus:

Oh wo, Jol-ly Mon sing.

Oh wo,
Make O-ri-on ring.
Make the mu-sic ring.
Give them ev-'ry-thing.

Verses:
2. And they
3. He was

Verse: 4. "Jolly Mon we know you; sing your last song very well."
They tossed him in the ocean 'cause their hearts were made in hell.
Came along a dolphin; he said, "Jolly Mon, hello,
I've always loved your singing. Climb on board, and don't let go."
Chorus:

Verse: 5. The night was filled with magic as they bid the sea good-bye.
They swam into the heavens; they stayed up in the sky.
And all the island people when they wish upon a star,
See the dolphin and the Jolly Mon who tell them where they are.
Chorus: